Outsmart
Test Anxiety

Have you ever studied super hard for a big test—read the material inside and out, maybe even made flashcards that you memorized until you dreamed about them—only to flop when the test came?

You might be surprised to learn you're not the only one! A lot of students experience test anxiety, which is what happens when nerves take over knowledge and cause you to freeze up during an exam, no matter how ready you might be to take it.

In the thought bubbles below, write some feelings you have when you take a test.

Remember a time you were anxious before a test, then answer the questions in the chart below (continues on the next page):

How many hours of sleep did you get the night before your test? Did you feel sleepy or wide awake?	
What did you eat for breakfast the morning of your test?	
What were you feeling on the day of your test? Were your thoughts positive or negative?	
When you got your test, did you believe you could do well or did you talk yourself out of success?	
How did you feel after taking your test?	

Do you wish you'd done anything differently?	
What grade did you receive on your test?	
Do you think you could've done better?	

What things do you notice from your answers in the boxes above that might affect how you feel about or perform on a test?

_____

_____

_____

_____

_____

_____

What do you think you could change to prevent anxiety when you take a test?

_____

_____

_____

_____

What is the worst thing that could happen when you fail a test?

_____

_____

_____

_____

What is the worst thing that could happen when you fail a test?

_____

_____

_____

_____

Sometimes, our fears are bigger than our reality. When test anxiety sets in, our fears can seem enormous compared to the actual consequences of not doing well on a test. Use the chart below to compare imagined fears with real consequences.

Anxiety tells me:	Reality tells me:

In the shapes below, draw what your anxiety about tests looks and feels like, and then what the reality of tests looks an feels like.

Anxiety:

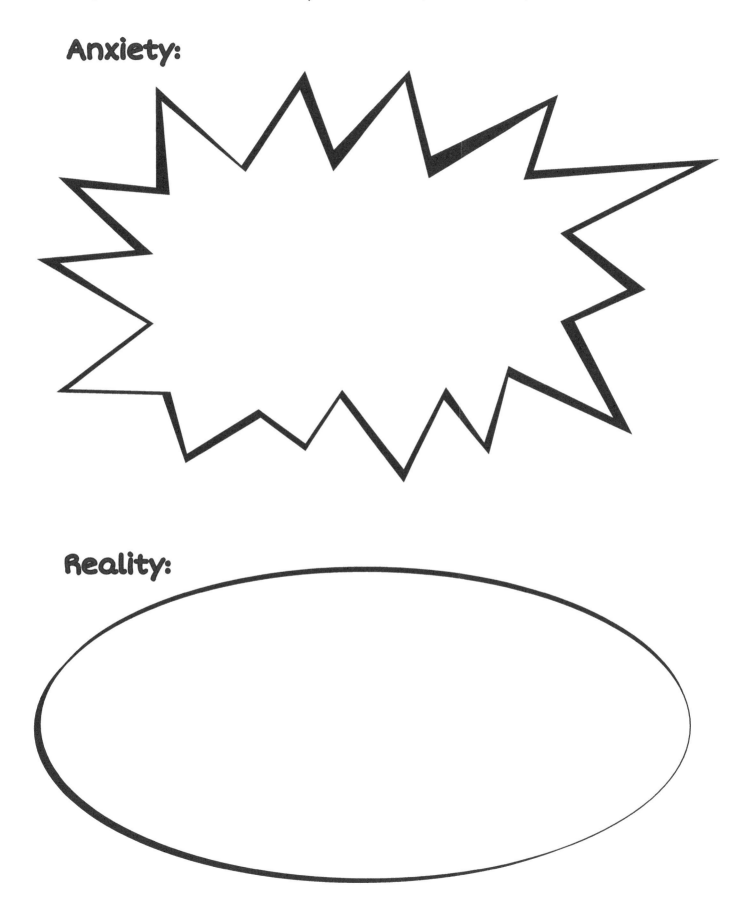

Reality:

Some kids have more anxiety in certain subjects or on certain types of tests. Pinpointing what makes you the most anxious can help you to equip yourself to beat your anxiety. Fill in your classes/subjects in the chart below. Then, on a scale of 1 to 5 (5 being most anxious), rate how anxious a test, in each subject, usually makes you.

Subject	Anxiety Level				
	1	2	3	4	5
	1	2	3	4	5
	1	2	3	4	5
	1	2	3	4	5
	1	2	3	4	5
	1	2	3	4	5
	1	2	3	4	5

Do some subjects make you more anxious than others? If so, why do you think that is?

_____

_____

_____

What can you do to be more successful in those particular areas?

_____

_____

_____

Now do the same thing for different types of tests or test questions.

Subject	Anxiety Level				
Multiple choice	1	2	3	4	5
Short answer	1	2	3	4	5
Essay	1	2	3	4	5
Timed test	1	2	3	4	5
Oral exam	1	2	3	4	5
Reading comprehension	1	2	3	4	5
Listening test	1	2	3	4	5
Other:	1	2	3	4	5

Do some types of tests make you more anxious than others? If so, why do you think that is?

_____

_____

_____

What can you do to be more successful in those particular areas?

_____

_____

_____

Ask your teacher for more practice questions of the type that's most difficult for you. Practicing these types of questions before the test will make you more comfortable.

One reason kids experience test anxiety is because they feel pressure from their parents to do well in school. Most parents care a lot about education, and want their children to do well. Sometimes, this means they put too much pressure on their child to succeed.

How do your parents feel about your schoolwork?

_____

_____

_____

_____

Do you feel like your parents put too much pressure on you?

_____

_____

_____

_____

Do your parents' words and actions tend to make you feel better or worse about your test anxiety?

_____

_____

_____

_____

In the circles below are adjectives that describe how some kids feel when it comes to their parents and the pressure of schoolwork and tests. Color the words that describe how you feel. If you have other feelings that aren't listed, add them. "When it comes to schoolwork, my parents make me feel."

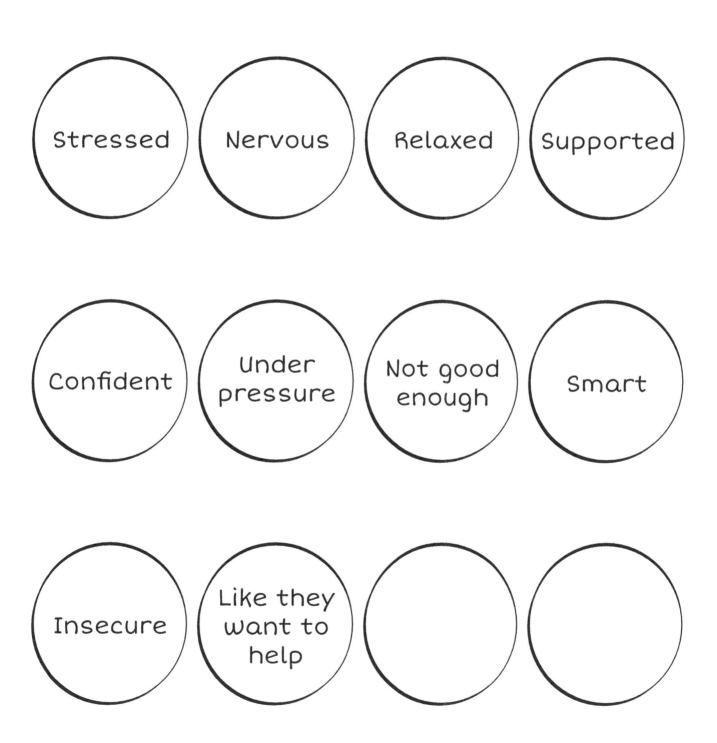

Most parents want their children to do well, and they try to help them be successful. But some parents just don't know the best ways to help their child do his or her best. Sometimes, parents do or say things that are very helpful, but other times they can do or say things that can actually make you feel worse, even if they don't mean to.

In the boxes below, write or draw things your parents do or say that are both helpful and unhelpful when it comes to your schoolwork and test anxiety.

Ways My Parents Help Me:

Unhelpful Things My Parents Do:

Most children don't know how to start a discussion about test anxiety, but the truth is, it can help to talk to your parents about how their actions and attitudes about your schoolwork make you feel. Now that you've written your feelings about your test anxiety, write some things you'd like to share with your parents in the speech bubble below.

How do you think your parents will respond once they understand you're experiencing test anxiety?

_____

_____

_____

_____

_____

Sometimes pressure can also come from other kids. Everyone has a tendency to compare themselves to their peers, but your test is about YOUR learning—not your classmates'! In the thought bubbles below, write things you've said or thought when comparing yourself to your peers. In the boxes, write something you can say to remind yourself it's not about them. Keep your thoughts positive and focused on your own improvement—not everyone else's.

It can also help to talk to your teacher about your test anxiety. Your teacher may have some ideas to ehlp make the experience less stressful for you, or to help you be more prepared. Some kids have a hard time talking to their teachers about their test anxiety, but don't be afraid. Your teacher is there to help you!

Draw a picture of yourself taking a test in the box below.

Read Measure your anxiety in the picture you drew on the previous page. Circle the number closest to how you usually feel when you take a test, with 0 being no anxiety at all and 10 being really high anxiety.

0   1   2   3   4   5   6   7   8   9   10

Now, measure the anxiety level you usually feel when you're studying a few days.

0   1   2   3   4   5   6   7   8   9   10

What's your anxiety level when you learn new material in class?

0   1   2   3   4   5   6   7   8   9   10

What school activities do you do that keep you in the 0-to-3 range?

1. _____
2. _____
3. _____
4. _____

What school activities do you do that keep you in the 4-to-8 range?

1. _____
2. _____
3. _____
4. _____

Draw a picture in the box below of something you chose from the 0-to-3 range.

Test anxiety is the result of your fear, stress, and negative thoughts combining to work against you. Read the following De-Stress Checklist below and check off the things you can try to reduce your test anxiety.

De-Stress Checklist:

☐	Good night's sleep
☐	Study as much as possible
☐	Believe you can do it
☐	Breathe deeply and slowly before taking the test
☐	Expect the best possible outcome
☐	Squash down fear by remembering that the worst outcome probably won't happen
☐	Talk to your parents and teacher about your test anxiety
☐	Eat a healthy snack before the test for extra brain power
☐	Think at least 10 positive thoughts before taking the test
☐	Allow yourself one full minute to process your worries. Then, think only good thoughts and about only positive outcomes.
☐	Reward yourself at the end of the test for doing the best job you could.

Next time you take a test, try some of the things on the
checklist from the previous page. Then, write about the
outcome below to keep track of what worked for you.

_____

_____

_____

_____

_____

_____

_____

_____

My favorite strategy from the list was _____

_____

because _____

_____

_____

_____

What positive thoughts did you use to reduce your test anxiety? Write them in the thought bubbles below.

Building Blocks to Success

In each block below, a tip is listed to help you be more successful when taking a test. Read each block and color those you find most helpful.

Read the test before starting to answer any questions.

Don't worry about order. Answer the questions you know best right away.

Budget your time wisely. Don't spend too much time on a question you don't know how to answer.

When answering short-answer or essay questions, include as much information as possible. Partial credit is better than none!

If you feel you need more time, talk to your teacher about it. If you feel you could do better by answering orally, talk to your teacher.

Breathe deeply and remind yourself that you can do this. It is 90 percent mental.

Try these steps on your next test and see how your anxiety improves. Measure your new anxiety level on the number chart below.

0 1 2 3 4 5 6 7 8 9 10

Studying for Success

A big part of passing a test is studying for success. Many times, when we're anxious about something, like a test, we do our best to avoid it. Have you ever noticed that when you have a test coming up, you'd rather clean your room than study? Have you ever sat down at the computer to read an online chapter for your test only to find yourself playing videogames or chatting on social-networking sites?

Time management and distraction play a big part in test success.

Use the chart below to fill in times you'll sit down and study in the days leading up to the test. Then make sure you stick to it!

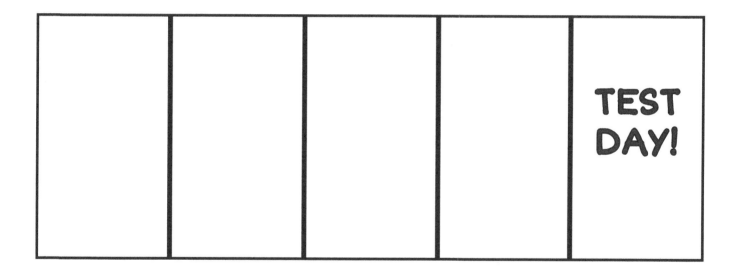

TEST DAY!

Getting Organized

Staying organized can help you be better prepared when test time comes. Below are some organizational strategies. Put a checkmark next to the ones you already practice, and a plus sign next to new ones you think you can try. Add your own ideas to the bottom of the list.

	Keep all your notes for each chapter together and in order.
	When you're teacher says, "This will be important for the test," make a note of it.
	Create a schedule for studying.
	Review earlier material from the chapter as you go along instead of waiting until test time.
	Highlight and/or color code your text or notes.
	Keep a list of important vocabulary.
	Make yourself checklists of everything you need to do or remember.

Study Time

There are many different ways to study, and no single right way to do it. Different things work for different kids. You need to try many ways of studying until you find what works best for you! In the triangles below are some different ways to study. If you've used other strategies that aren't listed, add them to the empty triangles.

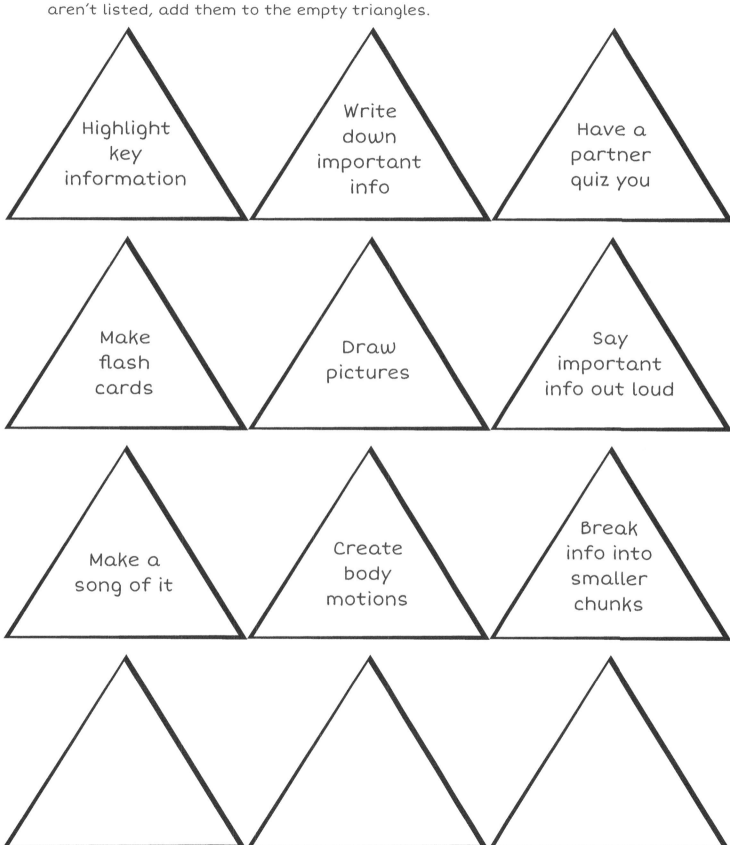

Highlight key information

Write down important info

Have a partner quiz you

Make flash cards

Draw pictures

Say important info out loud

Make a song of it

Create body motions

Break info into smaller chunks

Look at the triangles on the previous page and do the following:

1. Circle the ones you have used before.
2. Color the ones that have helped you.
3. Put a square around any new ones you want to try.

What are your favorite ways to study? Some children do best when they just read the material they need to learn. Some children need to do something active to remember facts. Some children need to write things down to remember them. What are you going to do to make sure you're studying for success?

_____

_____

_____

_____

_____

_____

_____

_____

                             _____

                             _____

                             _____

                             _____

                             _____

                             _____

Break Time

Putting in enough time studying is very important, but sometimes you also need to take breaks to help yourself relax. In the boxes below, write or draw some things you can do to relax.

Imagining yourself being successful is a great first step in getting there! Earlier, you drew how you usually look and feel while taking a test. Now, draw yourself being successful on a test. Keep this image in mind the next time you take a test. This will help set yourself up for success.

Taking a test is a way to measure how much knowledge you've retained about a certain subject. It does NOT measure who you are as a person! In the box below, draw a picture of who you are without a letter grade.

When you're having test anxiety, it can help to remember all the positive things about yourself. In the banners below, write five good things about yourself.

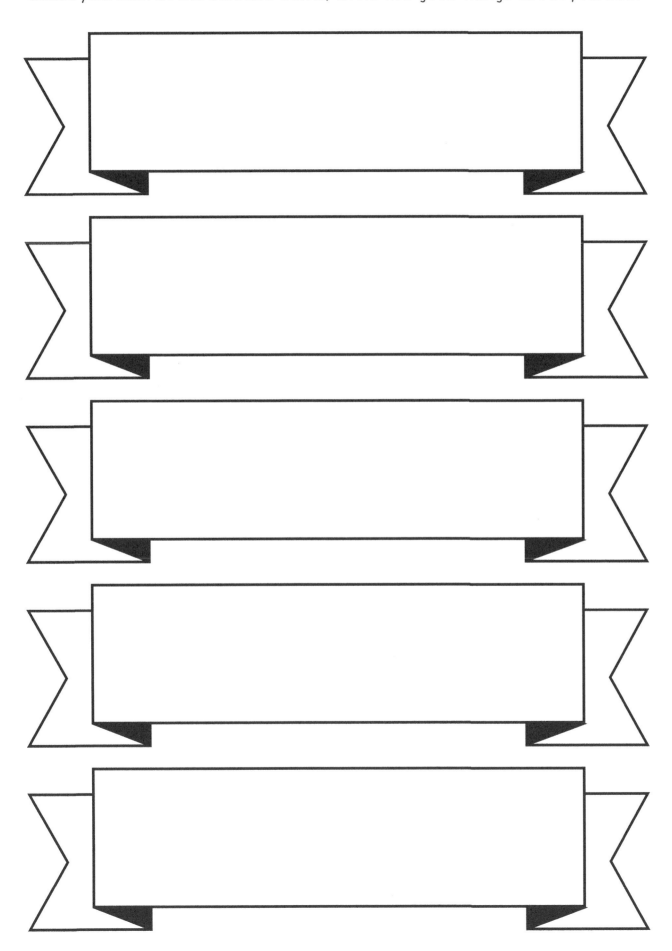

Support System

There are lots of people who support you and want to see you succeed. These could be family members, friends, teachers, counselors, or others. When you've got a test coming up, you can ask these people for help. You can talk to them about your anxiety, so they can help reassure you and build your confidence. Some of them might also be willing to help you study. They are your support system!

In the hearts below, write the names of people in your support system.

Read the poem below. Underline the lines that apply to you when you take a test. At the bottom of the page, sketch an image of someone stressing out over taking a test.

I Do Not Stress

When I try to take a test

My brain becomes a jumbled mess.

I try to remember all the facts

I try to breathe and just relax.

I try to answer every page

But the questions make me rage.

I make myself calm all the way down

And breathe slowly in and out.

I focus on the facts I know

And pass over the ones I don't.

Eventually I get through the test

And I know I've done my very best.

What matters most is I DO NOT STRESS!

Let's try to let all those anxious feelings out. In the box below, write, draw, or color something to represent your anxiety and other feelings about tests. When you're done, draw this symbol  over your picture to show that anxiety doesn't have a hold on you!

On each of the stars below, write a way you've learned to manage and overcome test anxiety.

You should be proud of yourself — you're coming a long way in learning to deal with your test anxiety. Your anxiety won't go away overnight, but as you learn strategies to deal with it, it will have less and less power over you. You're becoming stronger! Write a letter to yourself. When you're feeling worried about a test, pull this letter out and read it as a reminder of how great you are and everything you've learned about overcoming your anxiety.

Dear _____

_____

_____

_____

_____

_____

_____

_____

_____

_____

Love,

_____

Put your name in the star to remind yourself that YOU are AWESOME!

Great job! You've made it through this book and learned a lot about yourself and how to deal with your test anxiety. Keep this book to help you remember. Take it out whenever you need a reminder about all the great strategies you've learned to help you feel more prepared, more confident, and less worried when test time comes.

color me
HAPPY

HOW TO USE THIS REFLECTION JOURNAL

Now that you've completed the activities in this workbook, it's time to focus on putting everything you learned into practice.

What does that mean? It means using the things you've learned to help you each day.

Make a plan for each morning; then at the end of the day, before bedtime, think about your day.

What was good about it?
What brought you joy?
What went wrong?
How did you handle it?
What can you do to have a great day tomorrow?

HOW TO USE THIS REFLECTION JOURNAL

STEP 1: Each morning make a plan for your day by completing Side 1 of that day's journal page.

STEP 2: Each evening complete side 2 as you reflect on your day.

DATE: S M T W TH F S ___/___/___

ONLY POSITIVE THOUGHTS IN MY DAY
I can make today awesome by:

_____

_____

_____

DRAW IT!

what are you looking forward to most today?

I LOVE MYSELF
LIST 3 THINGS YOU LOVE ABOUT YOURSELF

WHAT IS SOMETHING THAT MAKES YOU HAPPY

_____

_____

_____

TODAY I FELT

SOMETHING GREAT THAT HAPPENED TODAY

_____

_____

_____

 THIS PERSON BROUGHT ME JOY TODAY

_____

_____

DATE: S M T W TH F S ___/___/___

ONLY POSITIVE THOUGHTS IN MY DAY
I can make today awesome by:

_____

_____

_____

DRAW IT!

what are you looking forward to most today?

I LOVE MYSELF
LIST 3 words that describe you

_____

_____

_____

TODAY I FELT

☺ ☺ 😐 ☹ 😖 😴

SOMETHING GREAT THAT HAPPENED TODAY

_____

_____

_____

THIS PERSON BROUGHT ME JOY TODAY

_____

_____

DATE: S M T W TH F S ___/___/___

ONLY POSITIVE THOUGHTS IN MY DAY
I can make today awesome by:

_____

_____

_____

DRAW IT!

what are you looking forward to most today?

I LOVE MYSELF
LIST 3 THINGS you are really good at doing

WHAT IS ONE OF YOUR FAVORITE MEMORIES

_____

_____

_____

TODAY I FELT

SOMETHING GREAT THAT HAPPENED TODAY

_____

_____

_____

 THIS PERSON BROUGHT ME JOY TODAY

_____

_____

DATE: S M T W TH F S ___/___/___

ONLY POSITIVE THOUGHTS IN MY DAY

I can make today awesome by:

_____

_____

_____

DRAW IT!

what are you looking forward to most today?

I LOVE MYSELF

LIST 3 THINGS YOU LOVE DOING

WHO IS A PERSON YOU ADMIRE (LIKE)

_____

_____

_____

TODAY I FELT

😄 🙂 😐 🙁 😣 😴

SOMETHING GREAT THAT HAPPENED TODAY

_____

_____

_____

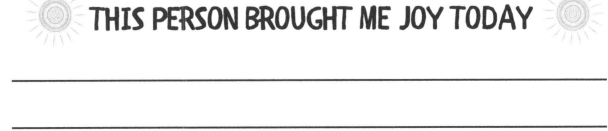 THIS PERSON BROUGHT ME JOY TODAY

_____

_____

DATE: S M T W TH F S ___/___/___

ONLY POSITIVE THOUGHTS IN MY DAY
I can make today awesome by:

_____

_____

_____

DRAW IT!

what are you looking forward to most today?

I LOVE MYSELF
LIST 3 THINGS YOU'D LIKE TO improve about yourself

WHAT IS SOMETHING THAT MAKES YOU PROUD?

_____

_____

_____

TODAY I FELT

😊 🙂 😐 🙁 😖 😴

SOMETHING GREAT THAT HAPPENED TODAY

_____

_____

_____

THIS PERSON BROUGHT ME JOY TODAY

_____

_____

DATE: S M T W TH F S ___/___/___

ONLY POSITIVE THOUGHTS IN MY DAY

I can make today awesome by:

_____

_____

_____

DRAW IT!

what are you looking forward to most today?

I LOVE MYSELF

LIST 3 THINGS THAT BRING YOU HAPPINESS

WHO IS THE KINDEST PERSON YOU KNOW

TODAY I FELT

SOMETHING GREAT THAT HAPPENED TODAY

 THIS PERSON BROUGHT ME JOY TODAY

DATE: S M T W TH F S ___/___/___

ONLY POSITIVE THOUGHTS IN MY DAY
I can make today awesome by:

_____

_____

_____

DRAW IT!

what are you looking forward to most today?

I LOVE MYSELF
WRITE 3 WORDS TO DESCRIBE YOUR LIFE

DID I TRY SOMETHING NEW TODAY?

_____

_____

_____

TODAY I FELT

😊 🙂 😐 ☹️ 😖 😴

SOMETHING GREAT THAT HAPPENED TODAY

_____

_____

_____

THIS PERSON BROUGHT ME JOY TODAY

_____

_____

DATE: S M T W TH F S ___/___/___

ONLY POSITIVE THOUGHTS IN MY DAY
I can make today awesome by:

_____

_____

_____

DRAW IT!

what are you looking forward to most today?

I LOVE MYSELF
LIST 3 THINGS WORDS TO DESCRIBE YOUR FAMILY

DID I GET OUT OF MY COMFORT ZONE TODAY?

_____

_____

_____

TODAY I FELT

😊 🙂 😐 🙁 😣 😴

SOMETHING GREAT THAT HAPPENED TODAY

_____

_____

_____

 THIS PERSON BROUGHT ME JOY TODAY

_____

_____

DATE: S M T W TH F S ___/___/___

ONLY POSITIVE THOUGHTS IN MY DAY

I can make today awesome by:

_____

_____

_____

DRAW IT!

what are you looking forward to most today?

I LOVE MYSELF

LIST 3 THINGS YOU LOVE ABOUT YOURSELF

THIS IS WHAT I COULD HAVE DONE BETTER TODAY

_____

_____

_____

TODAY I FELT

SOMETHING GREAT THAT HAPPENED TODAY

_____

_____

_____

 THIS PERSON BROUGHT ME JOY TODAY

_____

_____

DATE: S M T W TH F S ___ / ___ / ___

ONLY POSITIVE THOUGHTS IN MY DAY
I can make today awesome by:

_____

_____

_____

DRAW IT!

what are you looking forward to most today?

I LOVE MYSELF
LIST 3 THINGS THAT MAKE YOU SMILE

_____

_____

_____

TODAY I FELT

SOMETHING GREAT THAT HAPPENED TODAY

_____

_____

_____

THIS PERSON BROUGHT ME JOY TODAY

_____

_____

DATE: S M T W TH F S ___/___/___

ONLY POSITIVE THOUGHTS IN MY DAY
I can make today awesome by:

_____

_____

_____

DRAW IT!

what are you
looking forward
to most today?

I LOVE MYSELF
WRITE 3 THINGS THAT ARE GREAT ABOUT YOU

WHAT I'M LOVING ABOUT LIFE RIGHT NOW

_____

_____

_____

TODAY I FELT

SOMETHING GREAT THAT HAPPENED TODAY

_____

_____

_____

 THIS PERSON BROUGHT ME JOY TODAY

_____

_____

DATE: S M T W TH F S ___/___/___

ONLY POSITIVE THOUGHTS IN MY DAY
I can make today awesome by:

_____

_____

_____

DRAW IT!

what are you looking forward to most today?

I LOVE MYSELF
NAME 3 PEOPLE WHO BRING YOU HAPPINESS

I HOPE TOMORROW LOOKS LIKE THIS

_____

_____

_____

TODAY I FELT

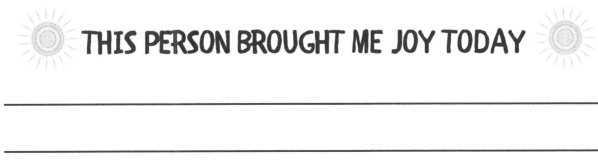

SOMETHING GREAT THAT HAPPENED TODAY

_____

_____

_____

THIS PERSON BROUGHT ME JOY TODAY

_____

_____

DATE: S M T W TH F S ___/___/___

ONLY POSITIVE THOUGHTS IN MY DAY
I can make today awesome by:

_____

_____

_____

DRAW IT!

what are you looking forward to most today?

I LOVE MYSELF
NAME 3 THINGS YOUR FRIENDS THINK YOU ARE AWESOME AT

TOMORROW I WILL SHOW KINDNESS TO THIS PERSON

_____

_____

_____

TODAY I FELT

SOMETHING GREAT THAT HAPPENED TODAY

_____

_____

_____

 THIS PERSON BROUGHT ME JOY TODAY

_____

_____

DATE: S M T W TH F S ___/___/___

ONLY POSITIVE THOUGHTS IN MY DAY
I can make today awesome by:

_____

_____

_____

DRAW IT!

what are you looking forward to most today?

I LOVE MYSELF
WRITE 3 THINGS YOUR CLASSMATES SAY YOU ARE GREAT AT

_____

_____

_____

TODAY I FELT

SOMETHING GREAT THAT HAPPENED TODAY

_____

_____

_____

THIS PERSON BROUGHT ME JOY TODAY

_____

_____

DATE: S M T W TH F S ___/___/___

ONLY POSITIVE THOUGHTS IN MY DAY
I can make today awesome by:

_____

_____

_____

DRAW IT!

what are you
looking forward
to most today?

I LOVE MYSELF
LIST 3 THINGS YOU DO THAT MAKES YOUR FAMILY HAPPY

TODAY I.....

_____

_____

_____

TODAY I FELT

😊 🙂 😐 🙁 😣 😴

SOMETHING GREAT THAT HAPPENED TODAY

_____

_____

_____

THIS PERSON BROUGHT ME JOY TODAY

_____

_____

DATE: S M T W TH F S ___/___/___

ONLY POSITIVE THOUGHTS IN MY DAY
I can make today awesome by:

_____

_____

_____

DRAW IT!

what are you looking forward to most today?

I LOVE MYSELF
LIST 3 THINGS THAT MAKE YOU HAPPY

_____

_____

_____

TODAY I FELT

SOMETHING GREAT THAT HAPPENED TODAY

_____

_____

_____

 THIS PERSON BROUGHT ME JOY TODAY

_____

_____

DATE: S M T W TH F S ___/___/___

ONLY POSITIVE THOUGHTS IN MY DAY
I can make today awesome by:

_____

_____

_____

DRAW IT!

what are you looking forward to most today?

I LOVE MYSELF
LIST 3 THINGS THAT MAKE YOU FEEL GOOD

TODAY I WANT TO.....

_____

_____

_____

TODAY I FELT

SOMETHING GREAT THAT HAPPENED TODAY

_____

_____

_____

THIS PERSON BROUGHT ME JOY TODAY

_____

_____

DATE: S M T W TH F S ___/___/___

ONLY POSITIVE THOUGHTS IN MY DAY

I can make today awesome by:

_____

_____

_____

DRAW IT!

what are you looking forward to most today?

I LOVE MYSELF

LIST 3 FUTURE GOALS FOR YOURSELF

TODAY'S ACTIVITIES MADE ME.....

_____

_____

_____

TODAY I FELT

😊 🙂 😐 ☹️ 😣 😴

SOMETHING GREAT THAT HAPPENED TODAY

_____

_____

_____

THIS PERSON BROUGHT ME JOY TODAY

_____

_____

DATE: S M T W TH F S ___/___/___

ONLY POSITIVE THOUGHTS IN MY DAY

I can make today awesome by:

_____

_____

_____

DRAW IT!

what are you looking forward to most today?

I LOVE MYSELF

LIST 3 THINGS YOU ENJOY DOING

TODAY I WANTED TO....

_____

_____

_____

TODAY I FELT

SOMETHING GREAT THAT HAPPENED TODAY

_____

_____

_____

THIS PERSON BROUGHT ME JOY TODAY

_____

_____

DATE: S M T W TH F S ___/___/___

ONLY POSITIVE THOUGHTS IN MY DAY
I can make today awesome by:

_____

_____

_____

DRAW IT!

what are you looking forward to most today?

I LOVE MYSELF
LIST 3 THINGS YOU DO THAT MAKES OTHERS SMILE

IF I COULD CHANGE THIS ABOUT TODAY

_____

_____

_____

TODAY I FELT

SOMETHING GREAT THAT HAPPENED TODAY

_____

_____

_____

THIS PERSON BROUGHT ME JOY TODAY

_____

_____

DATE: S M T W TH F S ___/___/___

ONLY POSITIVE THOUGHTS IN MY DAY

I can make today awesome by:

_____

_____

_____

DRAW IT!

what are you looking forward to most today?

I LOVE MYSELF

LIST 3 THINGS YOU LOVE ABOUT YOURSELF

MY DAY WAS.....

_____

_____

_____

TODAY I FELT

SOMETHING GREAT THAT HAPPENED TODAY

_____

_____

_____

THIS PERSON BROUGHT ME JOY TODAY

_____

_____

DATE: S M T W TH F S ___/___/___

ONLY POSITIVE THOUGHTS IN MY DAY
I can make today awesome by:

_____

_____

_____

DRAW IT!

what are you looking forward to most today?

I LOVE MYSELF
WRITE 3 AFFIRMATIONS: I AM.....

I LEARNED THIS ABOUT MYSELF TODAY

_____

_____

_____

TODAY I FELT

SOMETHING GREAT THAT HAPPENED TODAY

_____

_____

_____

THIS PERSON BROUGHT ME JOY TODAY

_____

_____

DATE: S M T W TH F S ___/___/___

ONLY POSITIVE THOUGHTS IN MY DAY

I can make today awesome by:

_____

_____

_____

DRAW IT!

what are you looking forward to most today?

I LOVE MYSELF

LIST 3 GOALS YOU'D LIKE TO ACHIEVE THIS WEEK

I HOPE TOMORROW IS....

_____

_____

_____

TODAY I FELT

☺ ☺ 😐 ☹ 😣 😴

SOMETHING GREAT THAT HAPPENED TODAY

_____

_____

_____

THIS PERSON BROUGHT ME JOY TODAY

_____

_____

DATE: S M T W TH F S ___/___/___

ONLY POSITIVE THOUGHTS IN MY DAY

I can make today awesome by:

_____

_____

_____

DRAW IT!

what are you looking forward to most today?

I LOVE MYSELF

LIST 3 THINGS YOU HAVE ALWAYS WANTED TO DO

LIFE IS GOOD BECAUSE...

_____

_____

_____

TODAY I FELT

SOMETHING GREAT THAT HAPPENED TODAY

_____

_____

_____

THIS PERSON BROUGHT ME JOY TODAY

_____

_____

DATE: S M T W TH F S ___/___/___

ONLY POSITIVE THOUGHTS IN MY DAY
I can make today awesome by:

_____

_____

_____

DRAW IT!

what are you looking forward to most today?

I LOVE MYSELF
LIST 3 THINGS YOU DREAM ABOUT

_____ IS MY HERO
BECAUSE.....

_____

_____

_____

TODAY I FELT

😊 🙂 😐 🙁 😣 😴

SOMETHING GREAT THAT HAPPENED TODAY

_____

_____

_____

THIS PERSON BROUGHT ME JOY TODAY

_____

_____

DATE: S M T W TH F S ___/___/___

ONLY POSITIVE THOUGHTS IN MY DAY
I can make today awesome by:

_____

_____

_____

DRAW IT!

what are you looking forward to most today?

I LOVE MYSELF
LIST 3 THINGS YOU HOPE TO DO THIS WEEK

TODAY I SMILED BECAUSE

_____

_____

_____

TODAY I FELT

SOMETHING GREAT THAT HAPPENED TODAY

_____

_____

_____

THIS PERSON BROUGHT ME JOY TODAY

_____

_____

DATE: S M T W TH F S ___/___/___

ONLY POSITIVE THOUGHTS IN MY DAY
I can make today awesome by:

_____

_____

_____

DRAW IT!

what are you looking forward to most today?

I LOVE MYSELF
LIST 3 THINGS YOU LOOK FORWARD TO

WHEN I FEEL MAD THIS IS WHAT I DO

_____

_____

_____

TODAY I FELT

SOMETHING GREAT THAT HAPPENED TODAY

_____

_____

_____

THIS PERSON BROUGHT ME JOY TODAY

_____

_____

DATE: S M T W TH F S ___ / ___ / ___

ONLY POSITIVE THOUGHTS IN MY DAY
I can make today awesome by:

_____

_____

_____

DRAW IT!

what are you looking forward to most today?

I LOVE MYSELF
LIST 3 THINGS YOU DID THAT YOU WERE PROUD OF DOING

I'M GRATEFUL FOR

_____

_____

_____

TODAY I FELT

😊 🙂 😐 ☹️ 😣 😴

SOMETHING GREAT THAT HAPPENED TODAY

_____

_____

_____

THIS PERSON BROUGHT ME JOY TODAY

_____

_____

DATE: S M T W TH F S ___/___/___

ONLY POSITIVE THOUGHTS IN MY DAY
I can make today awesome by:

_____

_____

_____

DRAW IT!

what are you looking forward to most today?

I LOVE MYSELF
LIST 3 THINGS YOU ARE EXCITED ABOUT

WHAT I'M LOVING ABOUT LIFE RIGHT NOW

_____

_____

_____

TODAY I FELT

SOMETHING GREAT THAT HAPPENED TODAY

_____

_____

_____

 THIS PERSON BROUGHT ME JOY TODAY

_____

_____

DATE: S M T W TH F S ___/___/___

ONLY POSITIVE THOUGHTS IN MY DAY
I can make today awesome by:

_____

_____

_____

DRAW IT!

what are you looking forward to most today?

I LOVE MYSELF
LIST 3 THINGS YOU ARE THANKFUL FOR

MY FAVORITE PERSON TO BE AROUND IS

_____

_____

_____

TODAY I FELT

SOMETHING GREAT THAT HAPPENED TODAY

_____

_____

_____

THIS PERSON BROUGHT ME JOY TODAY

_____

_____

DATE: S M T W TH F S ___/___/___

ONLY POSITIVE THOUGHTS IN MY DAY

I can make today awesome by:

_____

_____

_____

DRAW IT!

what are you looking forward to most today?

I LOVE MYSELF

LIST 3 WAYS YOUR LIFE IS AWESOME

THE PERSON I MOST ADMIRE IS

_____

_____

_____

TODAY I FELT

SOMETHING GREAT THAT HAPPENED TODAY

_____

_____

_____

 THIS PERSON BROUGHT ME JOY TODAY

_____

_____

DATE: S M T W TH F S ___/___/___

ONLY POSITIVE THOUGHTS IN MY DAY

I can make today awesome by:

_____

_____

_____

DRAW IT!

what are you looking forward to most today?

I LOVE MYSELF
LIST 3 THINGS YOU DID THIS WEEK

THIS IS WHAT BRINGS ME HAPPINESS

_____

_____

_____

TODAY I FELT

😊 🙂 😐 🙁 😖 😴

SOMETHING GREAT THAT HAPPENED TODAY

_____

_____

_____

THIS PERSON BROUGHT ME JOY TODAY

_____

_____

DATE: S M T W TH F S ___/___/___

ONLY POSITIVE THOUGHTS IN MY DAY

I can make today awesome by:

_____

_____

_____

DRAW IT!

what are you looking forward to most today?

I LOVE MYSELF

LIST 3 SMALL SUCCESS YOU HAD THIS WEEK

_____

_____

_____

TODAY I FELT

SOMETHING GREAT THAT HAPPENED TODAY

_____

_____

_____

 **THIS PERSON BROUGHT ME JOY TODAY**

_____

_____

DATE: S M T W TH F S ___/___/___

ONLY POSITIVE THOUGHTS IN MY DAY
I can make today awesome by:

_____

_____

_____

DRAW IT!

what are you looking forward to most today?

I LOVE MYSELF
LIST 3 THINGS YOU LIKE ABOUT YOURSELF

MY FAVORITE PART OF TODAY

_____

_____

_____

TODAY I FELT

😊 🙂 😐 ☹️ 😣 😴

SOMETHING GREAT THAT HAPPENED TODAY

_____

_____

_____

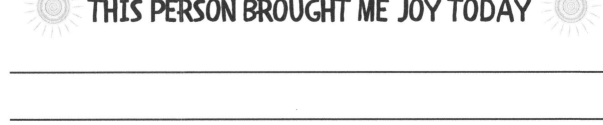 THIS PERSON BROUGHT ME JOY TODAY

_____

_____

DATE: S M T W TH F S ___/___/___

ONLY POSITIVE THOUGHTS IN MY DAY
I can make today awesome by:

_____
_____
_____

DRAW IT!

what are you looking forward to most today?

I LOVE MYSELF
LIST 3 WORDS THAT DESCRIBE YOU

WHAT I'M LOOKING FORWARD TO TOMORROW

_____

_____

_____

TODAY I FELT

SOMETHING GREAT THAT HAPPENED TODAY

_____

_____

_____

 THIS PERSON BROUGHT ME JOY TODAY

_____

_____

Made in United States
North Haven, CT
13 October 2022

25386395R00063